14¢	BUBBLE GUM	Giant Size	12¢
16¢	GUM DROPS		10¢
10¢	PEPPERMINTS	100 Size	32¢
19¢	JELLYBEANS		6¢

HEADACHE ?

ASPIRIN
Bottle of 100
39¢

SEED SALE! YOU PAY ONLY HALF PRICE

$1.00 VALUE — Full 2 Quart Capacity
Bottle 39¢ Limited Quantity

W9-ATT-712

Start a Workshop Now With NICKELDIME TOOLS

YOUR CHOICE!
$12.95 EA. ANY 2 for $25

HAND SAW

Finest tempered steel, Fulton quality, buy!
$1.89

HAMMER

98¢
Finest tempered steel, Fulton quality, buy!

NUTS and CANDY

ASSORTED
Homemaid Chocolates
A very delicious assortment of flavors. Pound 17¢

Salted Peanut Jumbos
1 Pound Cellophane Bag 16¢

Paper Shelled Pecans
All Clean and Perfect. Pound 25¢

Close-Out Price!
your chance to make a clean-up
25¢ PARSTEN'S TOOTH PASTE
3¼ oz. Tubes
13¢ 2 for 25c
Two for the regular price of one. Hurry! No more when it's gone.

9¢ WORM TRICK
These innocent looking pellets magically turn to worms when dropped in a glass of water. Horrify your friends with this harmless trick.

98¢ PHONY CAST
Imitation white plaster arm cast complete with arm sling. Looks like the real thing!

Secret Pocket "Pen" Radio
83¢ BATTERIES NEEDED. Ground wire included for best reception, but will work without grounding. Guaranteed to receive several stations, although reception will vary from place to place. Hear SPORTS, MUSIC, NEWS, etc. in office, school, bed, etc. Solid-state circuit. Complete, ready-to-play.

39¢

TRICK BLACK SOAP
Ordinary looking cake of soap until victim washes with it. Then his face turns blacker and blacker. Shocking! Harmless! A great trick.
32¢

34¢
THROW YOUR VOICE
Throw your voice into trunks, behind doors, everywhere. Fits in your mouth out of sight. Fool teacher, friends, family. Free book on "How to Become a Ventriloquist."

MINIATURE SECRET CAMERA
Precision camera so small, it fits in cigarette pack. Weighs 2½ ounces and takes 10 pictures per roll. Precision ground lens and time expose shutter. Can be hidden anywhere. Complete with free roll of film.
$1.69

21¢
JOY BUZZER
Windup novelty you wear like a ring. Your victim gets a "SHOCKING" hand shake. Absolutely harmless.

59¢
SKIN HEAD WIG
Most people try to grow hair. This is just the opposite. Made of flesh toned latex to fit all heads, really changes your appearance.

BOOMERANG 22¢
Something new in target throwing. In case you miss, it returns to you and bingo! you're set to "fire" again. Great fun and skill.

Buy One and Receive Extra Values

2 GLASSES OF Paste 34¢

Reg. 29c Size Puretest
ASPIRIN TABLETS
And a 25c Bottle
NASAL SPRAY
54c Value 39¢

FREE 25c Size Boodbury's Lotion
With a 50c Size Jar of
BOODBURY'S CREAM
For 34¢

50c Size
REXILLANA
COUGH SYRUP
And a 25c Box of
Cold Tablets
75c Value 50¢

Preserved **FIGS** IN SYRUP 40-Ounce Jar 49¢

1000 SHEETS
TOILET PAPER
OSWEGO BRAND 5 For 17¢

SAVE A JOB AND SAVE YOUR MONEY
69¢ in our February Sale
29c saving for 4 days only
SILVERTONE Alarm Clock
• Black
• Green
• Coral
• Ivory

Round or square case. Best seller at 98c.

GOODS

$1.98 Electric **Kitchen Wall Clock**
With Cord. Red — Green — IVORY.
$1.69

$1.09 Electric **Flat Iron**
COMPLETE WITH CORD
Sturdy — Long Life Heating Element
CLEARANCE SALE 94¢

ELECTRIC STOVE
• Polished chrome legs, long flexible cord, off-on switch.
89¢

Plastic Hen
1.99
Limited Quantity

35c SIZE **Freezone** FOR CORNS 22¢	50c SIZE **Pebeco Tooth Paste** 2 for 40¢
50c SIZE **Kolynos Toothpaste** 39¢	75c JAR **Molle Brushless** 48¢
50c **Dr. Lyons Tooth Powder** 32¢	J & J **TEK Tooth Brush** 23¢

48¢
Trick Dog 57¢
49¢

Clearance!
POUND JARS Charmona COLD CREAM
for very nearly ½ price
27¢

The very Charmona cream that you've been paying 45c for right

• Cross-Country Oil Books	$2.69
• 15-Plate Battery—2-yr. guarantee	$4.75
• Men's Work Shoes	$1.39
• Men's $2.98 Overshoes	$1.98
• Special—Sweat Shirts	59¢
• Bicycle Baskets	98¢
• Vacuum Bottles	66¢
• Lunch Boxes	39¢
• Alarm Clocks	88¢

★ CLOTHES PINS

Smooth selected hard wood. Stock up at this low price.
30 for 5¢

Curtain Stretcher

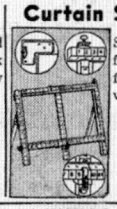

Strong, reinforced folding frame. A swell value!
89¢

CORN BROOM

Strong 5-sewed corn brooms, worth much more Limit!
19¢ ea.

MIXING BOWLS

Matched crystal . . brilliant pattern! Strong ribbed sides. Includes 6, 7½ and 9-inch bowls.
25¢ set

Buy **MASTER-MIXED PAINTS**
"TOP QUALITY ALWAYS" AT SUPER SAVINGS

SPECIAL! TURPENTINE, qt. 9c IN YOUR CONTAINER

Master-Mixed Housepaint	Gal. $2.85
Master-Mixed 4-Hr. Enamel	Qt. 98¢
5-Ft. Stepladder	Ea. 98¢
Master-Mixed Semi-Gloss	Qt. 89¢

• American Rag Rugs	79¢
• Cocoa Door Mats	89¢
• 812 Coil Spring Mattress	$17.88
• Carpet Sweepers	49¢
• Cannister Sets	29¢
• Ironing Boards	89¢
• Cafex-Coffee Maker—8-Cup	$2.98

Sale

NEW STYLE
SAUCE PANS
INTRODUCTORY PRICE
SET OF 3 $1.69 1-QT. 1½-QT. 2-QT.
3 COVERS TO FIT, 59c
The very latest in sauce pans, a slanting rim that's easy to clean. Also easy-clean corners. Made of thick sheet Aluminum for fast cooking, long wear. Cup markings. 3 handy sizes used often.

TRUE-FLAVOR **PERCOLATORS**
SPECIAL PRICES
$1.89 6-CUP
$1.98 8-CUP
OTHER SIZES ALSO ON SALE
America's favorite percolator. Now it's easy to make grand coffee every time. Handles are Bakelite.

BAKELITE HANDLE **SAUCE PANS**
INTRODUCTORY PRIC
$1.49 3-QT.
WITH COVER
OTHER SIZES ALSO ON SALE
Beautiful pans for modern kitchens, on sale for first time. Genuine Bakelite handles that stay cool.

LARGE SIZE **SAUCE POTS**
$2.29 8-QT
$2.69 10-QT.
NEW LOW PRICES
Needed in every kitchen for soup, boiled dinners, canning. Steam-seal keeps in goodness and flavors. Thick Aluminum heats quickly.

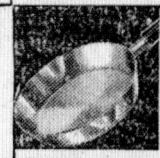

BAKELITE HANDLE **FRY PANS**
SPECIAL PRIC
$1.19 8-INC
OTHER SIZES ALSO ON SALE
Fried foods are "done to a turn" in this deep, thick pan. No hot spots. Browns evenly. Glossy Bakelite handle stays cool; won't turn in hand.

BEAUTIFUL **TEA KETTLES**
SPECIAL PRICE
$2.69 3-QT.
OTHER SIZES ALSO ON SALE
Styled for modern ranges and kitchens. Stationary handle for easy pouring. Non-slip Bakelite grip stays cool. Easy to fill.

NEW FANCY **RING MOLD**
INTRODUCTORY PRIC
75c
1¼-QUART CAPACIT
Round shape with beautiful swirl design on top. Molds attractive desserts, salads, etc. Resists stain. Same shape in small molds.

HANDY SAUCE POT SET
SPECIAL PRICE $5.25
2, 3, 4 and 6-QT. WITH COVERS
Matched set of pots for stewing, boiling, soup making. Sizes meet needs of every family. Thick Aluminum for quick, even heating.

4 Sue~J.P.L.
4 Aidan & Olive~V.F.

M enormously grateful 2 Pat, who was a perfect along the way. would like 2 thank Barbara Ensor 4 her invaluable insight, and Mary Sherwood & Jacquie Strasburger 4 their selective scrap scavenging. would like 2 thank David, Aidan & Olive 4 their advice & encouragement. M exceedingly grateful 2 Rachael Cole 4 her patience & craft, & 2 Anne Schwartz & Lee Wade 4 gleefully shoving me through doors hadn't even considered opening. –V.F.

Text copyright © 2010 by J. Patrick Lewis ✶ Illustrations copyright © 2010 by Valorie Fisher ✶ All rights reserved. Published in the United States by Schwartz & Wade Books, an imprint of Random House Children's Books, a division of Random House, Inc., New York. ✶ Schwartz & Wade Books and the colophon are trademarks of Random House, Inc. Visit us on the Web! www.randomhouse.com/kids ✶ Educators and librarians, for a variety of teaching tools, visit us at www.randomhouse.com/teachers

Library of Congress Cataloging-in-Publication Data ✶ Lewis, J. Patrick. ✶ The Fantastic 5 & 10 [cent] store : a rebus adventure / J. Patrick Lewis ; illustrated by Valorie Fisher. – 1st ed. ✶ p. cm. Title contains symbol for "cent." ✶ Summary: Rhymed text, featuring rebuses, describes the wonders of the store run by Mr. Nickel and Mrs. Dime. ISBN 978-0-375-85878-9 (trade) – ISBN 978-0-375-95878-6 (glb) ✶ 1. Rebuses. [1. Stories in rhyme. 2. Stores, Retail–Fiction. 3. Rebuses.] I. Fisher, Valorie, ill. II. Title. III. Title: Fantastic five & 10 [cent] Store. ✶ PZ8.3.L5855Fan 2010 ✶ [E]–dc22 ✶ 2008048827

The text of this book is set in Egizio. ✶ The illustrations are rendered in mixed-media collage. ✶ MANUFACTURED IN CHINA

10 9 8 7 6 5 4 3 2 1

First Edition

Random House Children's Books supports the First Amendment and celebrates the right to read.

The Fantastic 5&10¢ Store

A REBUS ADVENTURE

words by
J. Patrick Lewis

pictures by
Valorie Fisher

schwartz & wade books • new york

The  poured heat on  

,

Big  +s filled with 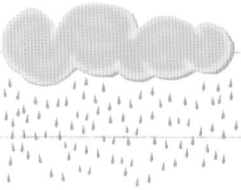 ,

As +flakes  +ed in+2 sleet.

The weather was insane!

But what  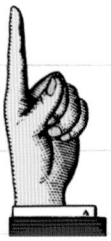 at the end of town

Nobody could X+  .

Pumpkin Street
BAKERY
Pasquale's
Barber Shop
Pumpkin Street
Cabl

The guessed "A of ."

The + ed, "A ?"

"A piece of ," the barber yelled,

"Has fallen from the SK+ !"

And so the guessing GAME went ON

Till each 1 had a r+ .

Pikin Street
Bakery

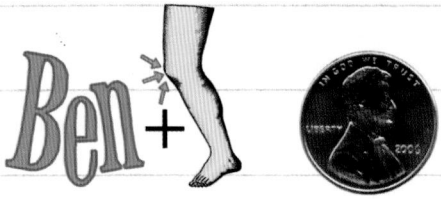

The 5&10¢ Store."

The  +come  hooted once,

So Ben+ 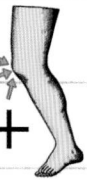 raised the latch.

He heard a funny thump-thump-thump,

And then a scritch & scratch.

When Ben+  entered,  +s

And 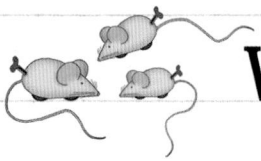 were playing  +ch.

Hoot
Please ask for assistance if you would like to see something in the window.
Mr. N. & Mrs. D.

The owner, Mr.  , spun

Round & round again.

"We have  had a customer

Since Mrs.  was 10!"

A 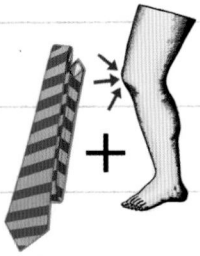 + 2+ba 2+ted TW+

And scared a plastic  .

SCOOP—and how! the miracle
EXTON HAIR BRUSH
Buy Now AT DEPARTMENT, HOUSEFURNISHINGS AND HARDWARE STORES
NUTS and CANDY
Homemaid Chocolates
500 SHEETS
CLEANSING TISSUES
ROAST
SALTED PEANUTS
$3.
REXILLANA
SHORTENING
BEANS
LIFE
Baseballs 99¢
$2.56
$1.99
50¢
Gum Gum
THERE ARE MANY OTHERS
VITAMIN CAPSULES
43¢
32¢
ALLSTATE
$2.99

A  with   + S

Flew over, popping 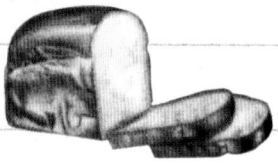 .

A  dipped itself in green,

+ ing the ceiling red.

And 2  could  W + 8 2 hit

A  on the  .

PAINT
Latex
Semi-gloss
Stir well before use.
Use a brush or roller.
HardHead
NAILS
NUTS
&
BOLTS
SCREWS
SACHEM
Braided Cotton

The  said 2 the saucer, "U

R quite a dish, m+ 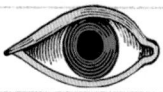 d+  !"

The calendar jumped off the 

 +cause it was leap y+  ,

 made a  

A  t+  .

Fresh Fru
Strawberr
Green Be
Grapefruit
87
BREWING BRIDGE
83
BRIEF CASE
1
25
FEBRUARY
MON TUES WED THURS FRI SAT
1 2 3
4 5 6 7 8 9 10
11 12 13 14 15 16 17
18 19 20 21 22 23 24
25 26 27 28 29

A 

and a 

bottle

From the 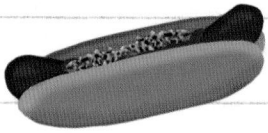 stand

Had flipped their lids & wobbled 2

The LITTLE Rubber  .

Said Mrs. 

, "And 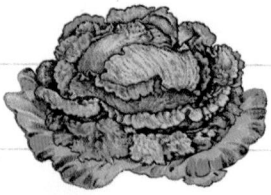 give

The 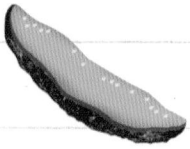  a 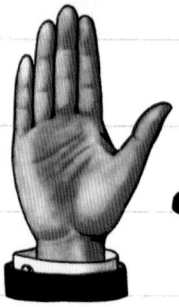 !"

Today's Specials
The Little Rubber Band
HOT DOG 85¢
CHILI DOG
CORN DOG 95¢
CHILI CHEESE DOG
BACON CHILI DOG $1.05
CAKE 55¢
PIE
MILKSHAKE 45¢
ICE CREAM
BACON EGGS
HAM EGGS
HOT CAKES
HAMBURGER
COFFEE
MILK
20¢
MUSTARD
BLUE LABEL TOMATO KETCHUP
S
P

A 

led a deck of  .

They marched in single file,

And shuffled 2 the  of  +s

 the Hardware 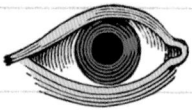 +  .

The  receiver told

The 

of 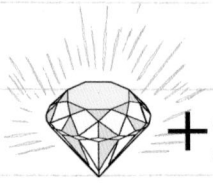 +s, "Dial!"

BOLTS
WASHERS
JOKER
JOKER
Q

Then Mrs.  said, "Ben+  , we

Think U R very wise.

Please  the  and  R+ 

And  who wins the prize.

We'll count on U, of course, 2 

The judge in case of  + S."

The  R+  + ed through the 5&10,

But soon the  led.

Cheer+  them on,  and  .

A  bounced on a 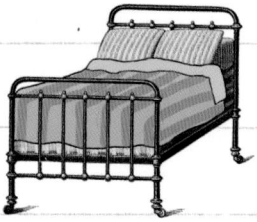 !

And at the finish  +ing line,

The  steamed a+  .

The tipping  2+ ted, "Whee!"

Accepting her award–

A  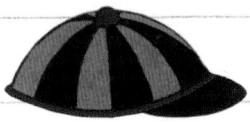 , a  , and

A LITTLE  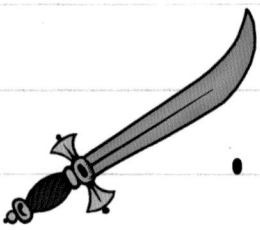 .

"Next R+  , the  twins!"

The napkin holder roared.

Baseballs 99¢

Still, Mr.   + ed a t +  ,

And Mrs.  wept 3.

"If only people came 2 shop,

We'd give them prizes, FREE!

Pink  + s, blue Hula Hoops–

How lovely would that  ?"

FOR RUN-DOWN BUDGETS
PRESERVES
15¢
MACARONI
SPAGHETTI
5¢
TRIANGLE
GREEN GIANT
DEL MAIZ
OVALTINE
PRESTO CAN
MALTEX
SHRIMP
BIG BOY
DINTY MOORE
SALADA
TEA
Baseballs 99¢
$1.99
50¢
$2.99

A  went off in Ben+  's  .

"I'll hang some twinkling 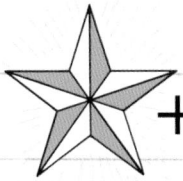 +s

 customers won't have 2 guess

At who & where   .

They'll come by  and  ,

By  ,  and  !"

Twinkling Stars
Twinkling Stars
Sparkle
Steel Wool
WASHERS
ECONOMY
SILVER POLISH
ZIP
WATER MIXED
GRINDING COMPOUND
McAleer's
POLISH

T
DIAMOND

And so they do. The  knocks,

The barber  +  the chime,

The  and the  , 2.

They 

in all the time

At the 1&5&10¢ Store–

THE    .

THE PENNYNICKELDIME
5&10

YOU CAN SAVE

50 Book Matches 5c

PINT SIZE VACUUM BOTTLE Regular 79c 67c

MEDIUM SIZE DISH SOAP Limit 12 5c

DISH CLOTHS Size 14×16 3 For 9c

ADJUSTABLE SHOE TREES For Men or Ladies 16c

125-FOOT ROLL WAX PAPER Heavy Type 14c

DORSET PLAYING CARDS Fancy Backs 19c

FACE CLOTHS Fancy Borders 6 For 29c

ROLL OF 100 Paper Towels 2 Rolls For 9c

$1.00 POCKET WATCH A Good Timepiece 87c

98c RUBBERSET SHAVING BRUSH Guaranteed Quality 83c

$2.50 VALUE BRIEF CASE With Zipper $1.98

100 Baby Brownie Camera 69c

100 FOLDING BED TRAY Adjustable For Reading 87c

1-POUND BAR CASTILE SOAP Made From Olive Oil 19c

BOX OF 12 PIN-APS Non-Chaffing 13c

MAGIC CARDS this price for a limited time only 29c

ELECTRICAL! — SPECIAL SALE — THE PENNINCKELDIME

Moderne Electric TOASTER • Black and Chrome • Mica Heat Element Reg. $1.09 94c

Reg. $1.79 HAIR DRYER • Hand Model • Complete With Cord • Ivory Finish $1.59

10c ALUMINUM SLICER • For Fruits • Eggs • Vegetables • Slices a Whole Egg with One Stroke. No muss, no fuss, no waste. 3-DAY SALE 8c

MECHANICAL PENCIL for the price of 2 postage stamps! 6¢ Choice of Colors • Genuine Bakelite • Precision Movement

LICORI CHOCO CHERR BUTTE

... The Fantastic 5&10¢ Store ...

A REBUS ADVENTURE WITHOUT THE REBUSES

The sun poured heat on Pumpkin Street,
Big buckets filled with rain,
As snowflakes barreled into sleet.
The weather was insane!
But what rose up at the end of town
Nobody could explain.

The butcher guessed "A leg of lamb."
The baker cried, "A pie?"
"A piece of cloud," the barber yelled,
"Has fallen from the sky!"
And so the guessing game went on
Till each one had a try.

"Why, it's a bus," the mailman said.
"Or else a dinosaur!"
"Nonsense," replied the doctor, "it's
A giant dresser drawer!"
Then Benny Penny shouted, "That's
The 5 & 10 Cent Store."

The welcome owl hooted once,
So Benny raised the latch.
He heard a funny thump-thump-thump,
And then a scritch and scratch.
When Benny Penny entered, cats
And mice were playing catch.

The owner, Mr. Nickel, spun
Round and round again.
"We have not had a customer
Since Mrs. Dime was ten!"
A tiny tuba tooted twice
And scared a plastic hen.

A toaster with flamingo wings
Flew over, popping bread.
A paintbrush dipped itself in green,
Painting the ceiling red.
And two nails could not wait to hit
A hammer on the head.

The cup said to the saucer, "You
Are quite a dish, my dear!"
The calendar jumped off the wall
Because it was leap year,
Which made a crocodile cry
A crocodile tear.

A mustard and a ketchup bottle
From the hot-dog stand
Had flipped their lids and wobbled to
The Little Rubber Band.
Said Mrs. Dime, "And let us give
The pickle jar a hand!"

A Joker led a deck of cards.
They marched in single file,
And shuffled to the Queen of Hearts
Down the Hardware aisle.
The telephone receiver told
The Jack of Diamonds, "Dial!"

Then Mrs. Dime said, "Benny, we
Think you are very wise.
Please watch the Pot and Teapot race
And see who wins the prize.
We'll count on you, of course, to be
The judge in case of ties."

The Pot raced through the 5 & 10,
But soon the Teapot led.
Cheering them on, balloon and flag.
A doll bounced on a bed!
And at the finish fishing line,
The Teapot steamed ahead.

The tipping Teapot tooted, "Wheee!"
Accepting her award—
A baseball cap, a yo-yo, and
A little pirate sword.
"Next race, the Salt & Pepper twins!"
The napkin holder roared.

Still, Mr. Nickel cried a tear,
And Mrs. Dime wept three.
"If only people came to shop,
We'd give them prizes, FREE!
Pink lollipops, blue Hula Hoops—
How lovely would that be?"

A light went off in Benny's head.
"I'll hang some twinkling stars
So customers won't have to guess
At who and where you are.
They'll come by train and tricycle,
By scooter, bus and car!"

And so they do. The doctor knocks,
The barber rings the chime,
The butcher and the baker, too.
They stop in all the time
At the 1 & 5 & 10 Cent Store—
The PennyNickelDime.

Doll House Furniture

Bathroom 95¢ — Nine metal pieces enameled orchid and white

Kitchen 95¢ — Seven metal pieces green lacquer and white finish

Bedroom 95¢ — Pink and blue enameled metal bed

1-Ounce SPIRITS CAMPHOR 12c

25c PLAYING CARDS Fancy Backs 13c

100 Tablets Finkle's 7

No filters to buy! No filters to change! Nothing to get broken!

Neva-Break ALUMINUM VACUUM Coffee Maker

Aluminum neva-break upper & lower bowls. Aluminum never-wear-out filter. Bakelite handle. Wide mouth lower bowl. Easy to clean! 8 Cup 1.98

There's Beauty in Every Drop TEEL for Teeth Liquid Dentifrice

Penetrates crevices between the teeth. Floats away decaying food particles. Med. size 23¢

SALE